WHITE SPOT

WHITE SPOT

MURRAY LEINSTER

WILDSIDE PRESS

WHITE SPOT

CHAPTER 1

THE PLANET did not look promising, but they had no choice. When a ship's drive blows between star systems, it has to be fixed. If metal parts must be recast and machined, and burned-out wiring has to be pieced together and insulated by hand, the job takes literally months. And if, then, getting home is a matter of more months of journeying with a drive that still limps, while coughing and cutting off for seconds or until it is tinkered with—why, the traveler has to find some way to renew his food supply.

It is for such occasions that the Interstellar Code requires all ships to carry an emergency kit with seeds and agricultural directions.

The *Danaë*, therefore, limped to the nearest Soltype star to hunt for a planet on which to plant some crops. There was Borden and his wife, Ellen. There was Sattell, whom they would be glad to part with when they got home. There was Jerry, who was diffident enough to be tolerable in spite of his lack of years. They were all at the forward vision port when they approached the only possible planet.

"It's fifty million miles out," Borden said. "A bit on the hot side. But the sun is smaller than Sol, so it may not be too bad. At least there are polar caps—small ones."

They went in closer, circling as they headed for atmosphere.

"No seas," Sattell said. "Pretty barren."

The others said nothing. It did not look at all encouraging.

The *Danaë* went in on a spiral descending orbit. Borden looked for other planets. He found a gas giant with a high

speed rotation. It was flattened, oblate. He checked it with

the two polar caps on the nearer world and said worriedly:

"If the ecliptic's where I think it is, there'll be no seasons to speak of. I was hoping this planet was near its equinox, because the icecaps are so nearly the same size."

Ellen said absorbedly, "I think I see a tinge of olive green around that icecap. The smaller one."

"Probably vegetation," agreed her husband. "But I don't see any more. The place does look to be mostly desert."

Then Jerry said: "Could that be ice, there?"

There was a white spot in the middle of the sandy-colored northern hemisphere. It was the size of a pin head to the naked eye. Borden swung a telescope on it. They were nearly above the point now, where day turned into night.

The sunlight fell upon the white spot at a flat angle. If the whiteness were perpetual snow on the tops of mountains, the mountains should cast shadows. But Borden could not make out shadows near the white. Automatically he snapped the telecamera before he gave up the effort to understand the white spot.

"I doubt it's snow," he said. "I don't know what it is."

"Surely you can make a guess!" said Sattell, with that elaborate courtesy which was getting on everyone's nerves.

"I can't," Borden said.

The ship moved to the dark side of the planet, and presently plunged into its shadow.

They went on, watching for lights. There were none. When they came out to sunlight again, they had descended a long way during their time in the planet's night.

They could see that the surface of the planet was pure tumbled sand dunes with occasional showings of stone. They were three-quarters of the way around when they saw the white spot again. This time they were no more than four or five hundred miles high. They could tell its size.

It was all of three hundred miles long, north and south, and from fifty to seventy-five miles wide. There were thin hairlines running from it, remarkably straight on the whole, to the north and south. They were very, very fine lines. The patch was still white. As they came to be in line between it and the sun, their shadow would have passed almost over it.

The white spot changed abruptly. One instant it was white, the next, a patch of it had turned silver. That silvery appearance spread out and out in a swift rippling motion. The patch became silver all over its entire surface.

Then it turned to flame.

There was a screaming of alarm gongs. The emergency feedback screens went on and everything went black outside. The lights in the ship dimmed down to mere dull red glows.

There was silence.

The ports showed blackness. The drive, of course, ceased to operate. The ship had sealed itself in a shell of screening, through which nothing at all could penetrate, but which drew upon the ship's power tanks for as much energy as it neutralized outside. And the drain was so great that the interior lights were dim red spots and not lights at all.

For five heartbeats the blackness persisted while the four in the ship stayed frozen.

The feedback screen cut off. Again they saw the planet below. The white patch once more was white, instead of flame. But as they looked, the silvery look spread out all over it in glittering ripples, and they seemed to look into the heart of a sun's ravening furnaces before the feedback screen came into existence for their defense. The ports were blacked out again.

The ship hurtled on toward emptiness. It was blind. It was helpless.

Borden moved an emergency light to shine on the output meter. The needle was fast against the pin. The feedback screen was not only drawing maximum safe power. It was working on an effective short circuit of the ship's entire power supply. Busbars carrying that current would be heating up. They would melt at any instant.

Borden's fingers moved swiftly. He set up a shunt for on-switch operation of the feedback field.

He threw the last cross-over tumbler and waited, with sweat beading his forehead. Something had flung a beam of pure heat energy at the *Danaë*. It should have volatilized the small spacecraft immediately, but it had been left on for four seconds.

When it ended, the feedback screen cut off too. Then the *Danaë* had been detected a second time and the planetary weapon used again. Now, with the feedback field on switch instead of relay, *if* the heat ray turned off again the feedback field wouldn't, and the *Danaë* should be indetectable to anything but a permeability probe. The spaceship would seem to have been destroyed, if the heat-beam went off before the ship's power failed.

It did. A relay clicked somewhere, cutting a current flow of some tens of thousands of amperes. The lights inside the ship flashed to full brightness. Borden's eyes flicked to the power meters. The operational power tank meter read zero. The emergency reserve power tank meter showed a reading that made fresh sweat come out on Borden's face.

But the ports stayed black. Absolutely any form of energy striking the feedback field outside would be neutralized. No light would be reflected. Any detector field would be exactly canceled, as if nothing whatever existed where the *Danaë* hurtled onward some few hundred miles above the planet's surface.

The *Danaë*, at the moment, was in the position of having made a hole about itself to crawl into. But it couldn't use its drive. It couldn't see out. It was hiding in blackness of its own creation, like a cuttlefish in its own ink.

"Dee," Ellen Borden asked her husband in a shaky voice, "what happened?"

"Something threw a heat ray at us," said Borden. He mopped his forehead. "We should have exploded to incandescent gas. But our feedback field stopped it. The heat ray cut off when we should have been destroyed— and so did our field, so there we were again! And so we got a second beaming. But now we aren't. At least we appear not to be. So we can live until we crash."

Sattell said in a suddenly high-pitched voice, "How long will that be?"

"I don't know the gravity," Borden told him. "But it does take time to fall four hundred miles. We have some velocity, too. It's under orbital speed but it'll help. I'm going to figure something out."

He swung in the control chair and hit keys on the computer. The size of the white spot. It had all turned silvery, then all of it had flamed. Why? The amount of power in the heat ray—a rough guess. Nobody could have figures on what a ship's tanks would yield on short circuit, but the field had had to neutralize some hundreds of megawatts of pure heat.

The amount of overlap—the size of the heat ray itself—was another guess and a wild one. And why had all of the white spot spat flame? Every bit of it? Three hundred miles by an average of sixty . . . Even at low power—

The computer clicked.

"Sun power," Borden said grimly, after a moment. "That figures out just about right. Not more than a kilowatt to the square yard, but eighteen thousand square miles has plenty of square yards! We've been on the receiving end of a sun mirror heat ray, and if it had been accurately figured we'd have fried." Then he said, "But a sun mirror doesn't work at night!"

He punched keys again. Presently he looked at his wrist chronometer. He waited.

"We're falling!" Sattell cried. "Do something!"

"Forty seconds more," said Borden. "I'm gambling your life, Sattell, but I'm gambling Ellen's and mine too, not to mention Jerry's. Calm down."

His eyes turned to the meter that showed the feedback field drain. It was drawing precisely the amount of power needed to cancel out the sunlight falling on it, as well as the starlight, and the light reflected from the day side of the world below them. That drain was less than it had been. They were crossing the planet's terminator—the line dividing the light side from the dark side—as they plunged toward the sandy deserts.

The drain dropped abruptly. They had moved into the planet's shadow. Into night.

Instantly, Borden flicked off the feedback field. His eyes darted to the nearest object radar dial. They were still sixty miles high, but falling at a tremendous speed. Borden's hands moved quickly over the controls. Lift. Full atmosphere drive on a new course.

"We won't crash," he said evenly, "unless we're shot at with something that works in the dark. But that sun mirror business is odd. There's only a certain size of sun mirror that's economical. When they get too big there are better weapons for the money. That one was big! So maybe it's the best weapon this planet has. In which case we'll be nearest safety at one of the icecaps. Sun mirrors will be handicapped in polar regions!"

"They—tried to kill us!" Sattell said, panting. "They don't like strangers! They fired on us without warning! We can't land on this planet! We've got to go on!"

"If you want to know," Borden told him, "we haven't any fuel to go on with. And we happen to be short of food. And did you remember—"

The ship's drive cut off. It had been burnt out and repaired by hand, with inevitable drawbacks. Since the repair, it had run steadily for as long as three days at a time. But also it had stopped four times in one hour, and it had needed tinkering with three times in one day.

It ought to be overhauled. For now it had cut off, and they were forty miles high. If it came on again they would live; if it didn't, they wouldn't.

After six spine-chilling seconds the drive came on again. Ten minutes later it went off for two seconds. Half an hour later it made that ominous hiccoughing which presaged immediate and final failure. But it didn't fail.

It was not pleasant to be so close to a planet they could not afford to leave, with a drive that threatened to give up the ghost at any instant, and with something on the planet which had used a sun mirror beam to try to volatilize the *Danaë* without parley. Apparently the four in the small ship had the choice of dying on this planet or not too far away in space.

They needed food, and they needed fuel. Above all, if the planet was inhabited, they needed friendship, and they weren't likely to get it.

They were only ten miles high when signs of dawn appeared ahead. Of course, if they happened to be moving with the planet's rotation, they'd be moving into sunset from the night. They didn't know. Not yet. But there were gray clouds ahead, to the right and below.

A little later they were five miles high and the clouds were still below. There was twilight ahead. At two miles altitude the drive hesitated for a moment, and caught again after all four in the control room had stopped breathing.

Red sunlight appeared before the ship in a spreading, sprawling thin line. At five thousand feet the ship had slowed to a bare crawl—a few hundred miles an hour. And the dawn came up like thunder.

CHAPTER 2

TO THE left and behind was desert, stretching away in the dawnlight, in every conceivable shade of tawny yellow and red, with blue shadows behind the hummocks in the sand, and with an utterly cloudless sky overhead. To the right and ahead was an area of straggling, stunted vegetation beneath rose-tinted cloud masses with the dazzling white of snow against the horizon. There were other clouds above the snow.

The drive burbled erratically. The ship dropped like a stone. Then the drive flickered on, and off, and on and off again so that ship's whole fabric shook.

Borden threw the drive off and on again and the induction surge of current cleared whatever was wrong for a moment. They felt the ship fighting wind pressure that was trying to turn it end over end. Then it steadied, and nothing happened—and still nothing happened.

The crash came violently. Ellen was flung against Borden and held fast to him. Jerry collapsed to the floor. Sattell went reeling and banged against the end wall of the control room.

There was stillness.

Borden stared at the screens, then got up painfully and went to a port. The ship had landed in soil which seemed to be essentially sand. It had splashed the soil aside in coming to ground. But it was not desert sand. There was moisture here. Beyond the impact area a straggling ground cover grew. It looked like grass, but it was not.

Nearby was one greenish object which looked like a cactus without its spines. It had a silky covering like down. A little farther on Borden could see three or four things quite like stunted, barkiess trees.

The ground was gently rolling. In the distance the growing light showed a whitish haze, and clouds in the sky. All shadows were long and stretched-out. This was not far from the icecap. Indeed, it appeared that snow was nearby. But from the port on the opposite side of the ship the beginning of the planetary desert could be seen.

"We're down," said Borden with relief. "Now we've got to find out if anybody saw us land, and if so, whether they'll insist on killing us or whether we can make friends."

Sattell said, "You've got to arm me, Borden! You can't leave me unarmed on a hostile planet!"

"I'd like to have four weapons ready instead of three, though if we have to fight a whole planet even four won't be much good. But I can't risk letting you have anything dangerous in your hands," Borden said.

Sattell ground his teeth.

Jerry said apologetically, "Shall I test the air, sir?"

Borden nodded. He regarded Sattell with a weary, worried frown, while Jerry readied the test. The situation was bad, but Sattell was troublesome too.

Two months ago, while the drive was still in process of repair, Borden had heard a strangled cry from Ellen. He found her struggling to scream as she fought Sattell.

Borden's appearance had ended the struggle, of course. Sattell had been confined to his bunk for two weeks before he was able to move about again. But Borden hadn't been able to kill an unconscious man then, and he couldn't kill Sattell in cold blood now. But Sattell could kill anybody. And he would, if he got the chance.

"It's the devil, Sattell," Borden said. "If I didn't think you were a rat I could make a bargain to forget what's happened until we get the ship safely home. But I don't think you'd keep a bargain."

Sattell snarled at him and turned away. Jerry looked up from the tiny air-testing cabinet. He'd drawn in a sample of outer air and a silent discharge had turned its oxygen to ozone, which a reagent absorbed. A hot silver wire stayed bright, and so proved the absence of chlorine or sulphur, CO_2 tested negligible, and hot magnesium took up nitrogen. The remnant of the sample did not react with reagent after reagent, so it had to be noble gases.

"It seems all right, sir," said Jerry. "If I may, I'll go in the airlock and take a direct sniff. May I, sir?"

"Unless Sattell wants to volunteer," Borden observed. "I would think better of you, Sattell, if you volunteered for first landing."

Sattell laughed. "Oh, yes! I'll walk out on a hostile planet, and let you take off and leave me! Even if you can't leave the planet, you can come down ten thousand miles away. You'd like to do that, too!"

"Meaning," Borden said, "that *you* would . . . All right, Jerry. Go ahead."

"Yes, sir." Jerry went out. They heard the inner airlock door open.

Borden said heavily, "It would be sensible to lock you up while we're aground, Sattell. I can't leave the ship with you inside and free. You've already said what you'd do if you could—take off and maroon us."

Jerry's voice came from the airlock through a speaker.

"Mr. Borden, sir, the air's wonderful! You don't realize what canned air is like until you breathe fresh again. Wonderful, sir! I'm going out."

Borden nodded to Ellen. She moved over to watch through a port as Jerry made the first landing on this unnamed planet of an unnamed sun. She could see the straggling ground-cover vegetation, and the thing that looked like a cactus except that it wasn't, and the trees. She saw Jerry step to the ground and look about, breathing deeply.

Behind her, Borden said bitterly,

"We were blasted at without challenge. But it was with a sun mirror that was not too efficient. The local race may not have any other power than sunlight. If so, they won't be up here by the icecap! If we weren't spotted by radar as we landed, we may make good repairs, raise food, and get back to space without our presence being known— because they should think they had wiped us out."

Ellen gasped suddenly from the port: "Dee! Natives! They've seen Jerry! They're coming close!"

Borden moved quickly to look over her shoulder. Sattell took a second port. They stared out at the strange world about the *Danaë*.

Jerry had kicked a hole in the sod and picked up a bit of it to examine. And, not sixty yards from him, three creatures were regarding him with intense curiosity.

They were furry bipeds. They stood as erect as penguins, not bending forward in the least. They had enormously long arms which almost reached to the ground beside them. From what should have been their chins, single tentacles drooped—like the trunk of an elephant, except that it was beneath the mouth opening instead of above it. They stared at Jerry with manifest mounting excitement, making gestures to each other with their trunks and arms.

Borden moved to warn Jerry through the outside speaker. But Jerry looked up directly at the creatures. He spoke to them in a quiet voice.

At the sound of his words their manner changed. Borden thought irrelevantly of the way a dog flattens his ears when his master speaks to him. But these creatures flattened all their fur. Jerry spoke again. He waved his hand. He glanced at the *Danaë*'s port and nodded reassuringly.

The three creatures moved hesitantly toward him. Two of them stopped some forty yards distant. One came on. Suddenly it wriggled with an odd effect of embarrassment. The flattening of its fur became more noticeable.

A fourth creature of the same kind came loping over a rise in the ground. It used its long arms to balance itself as an ape might do, but an ape does not run upright. This creature did. It saw Jerry and stopped short, staring.

The creature which had advanced toward Jerry appeared to be more and more embarrassed. Jerry moved to meet it. When he was ten feet away the creature lay down on the ground and rolled over on its back. It waved its trunk wildly, as if supplicating approval.

Jerry bent over and scratched the furry body as if he knew exactly what it wanted. The two others who had been its companions loped forward, plunged to the ground, rolled over on their backs and waved their trunks as wildly as the first. Jerry scratched them.

The fourth creature, which had stared wide-eyed, suddenly waved its arms and burst into a headlong rush. Its haste seemed frantic. It scuttled frenziedly, made a leap, turned over as it soared, landed on its back two yards from Jerry and slid to his feet.

When Jerry scratched it, it wriggled ecstatically. Its trunk waved as though it were experiencing infinite bliss.

Borden said slowly, "Something on this planet tried to burn us down with a heat ray not half an hour ago. We land—and this happens! What sort of place is this, anyhow?"

CHAPTER 3

IT WAS a queer place, they soon learned. The climate was cool, but pleasant. There were no radio waves beneath a readily detectable ionosphere. Yet apparatus over an area three hundred miles by an average sixty—the white spot—had responded in seconds; in parts of seconds.

Which meant electric control. Which implied radio. But there were no radio waves, which should have been proof that there was no civilization on this planet capable of doing what certainly had been done. Which was nonsense.

On the fourth day after landing there had been no alarm, but there was a good-sized group of furry bipeds always waiting hopefully about the *Danaë* for one of the humans to come out and scratch them. All but Sattell. When he came out of the *Danaë*, the bipeds moved away. They would not go near him.

"I am not comfortable," Borden said to Jerry. "Something drained power from us. Enough to run the ship for two years was drained out in eight seconds! But we land, and the only inhabitants are your fine furry friends whose one purpose in life seems to be to get scratched. They act more like pets than wild animals, and sometimes more like people than pets. But if they're pets, did their masters try to kill us? What does go on on this planet, anyhow?"

Jerry said modestly, "I'm beginning to understand the furry creatures a little, sir. They're remarkably intelligent, for animals. They want me to go somewhere with them. I'd like to. Is it all right?"

Borden said, "If you think it's safe. Ellen has the planting well under way, and the fuel synthesizer is working after a fashion, although I'd a lot rather have it working near the equator. I'm getting along fairly well with re-building our drive, but there's a long job ahead. If other planetary inhabitants don't find us and kill us, we're all right. Go along if you like, within reason. But I wish you could take Sattell with you."

That couldn't be done. The two-legged creatures hung about the ship wearing an air of happy anticipation when all the humans were inside, and flopping eagerly on their backs to be scratched, when they came out. But when Sattell tried to approach one of the creatures, they fled as if in terror. Not one had ever been knowingly within a hundred yards of him—and he hated them.

When Jerry first reported that they had some sort of language and could exchange simple facts—he didn't know whether they could exchange ideas or not—Sattell savagely insisted that those who knew of the existence of the ship should be killed, and any others who discov-ered it also killed. The idea would be to keep the news of the *Danaë*'s landing from reaching whatever other race might inhabit the white spot of the heat ray.

But there were always some of the furry ones around. Sometimes more, sometimes less. Maybe only the same ones came to the ship. Maybe they went away and others took their places. Neither Borden nor Jerry was sure, but both demurred at killing. Besides, the news had already gone as far as such creatures were likely to take it before Sattell proposed to wipe them out.

Sattell raged when he was overruled. He was over-ruled on most things because he couldn't be trusted. Bor-den wouldn't let him work on the drive. He might try to make sure that if he didn't get back to Earth, nobody else should, either.

Ellen took the dibble stick and the seed capsules and planted the crop that might supply them with food. Each seed was enclosed in a gelatine capsule with a bit of fertilizer and a spore culture of terrestrial soil microorganisms. Planted, by the time moisture reached the seed there was a bed of Earth's own microscopic soil flora around the seed to help it grow.

But Sattell couldn't be trusted to plant seed, either, if the others would benefit.

He couldn't even be allowed to work the fuel synthesizer. In that apparatus plain water entered a force field in which H_1 and H_2 simply could not exist as molecules or ions. So the atoms frantically absorbed heat energy from their surroundings to make pseudo valence bonds and develop giant hydrogen molecules which could only be written down as being of molecular weight.

The fuel synthesizer was set up a good half-mile from the space ship and was developing a small icecap of its own. But it would be a long time before there was drive fuel to refill the ship's tanks. Sattell might sabotage that.

So he had to be treated as the pampered guest of those who believed implicitly in his will to murder them. All arms were safely locked away. Even the airlock fastening had to be dismantled, so he couldn't lock everybody else out of the ship.

And Borden and Ellen and Jerry went armed, and had nerve-wrackingly to be on guard at all times. But it would have been ridiculous to confine Sattell so he had the status of a nonworking guest because he was a potential murderer.

There was not much for Jerry to do either, except hold conferences with his admirers. On the fifth twenty-hour day after the *Danaë*'s landing, Jerry set off with an excited mob of furry, trunk-waving friends. He carried a walkie-talkie, depending on the absence of radio waves from the planet's atmosphere to make its use safe.

Two hours after he had headed north toward the ice, Borden and Ellen came back from an inspection tour of the crops and fuel synthesizer, and found that Sattell had disappeared, too. He'd taken all the food he could conveniently carry from their depressingly short supply.

Borden swore. Sattell underfoot was a nuisance and a menace. But Sattell at large might be more, and worse. There was no glamor in being castaway on this alien world, such as is shown in visi-screen plays. The *Danaë* was a small utility ship, suitable for small expeditions for scientific purposes, or for the staking out of private planetary estates—a common practice, these days—and the servicing of such establishments.

Her eighty-foot length now rested slightly askew in the pit her landing had made. About her was arctic flora, and the thick fur of the bipeds suggested that they were arctic animals themselves. But here close to the icecap was the only place on this planet where a man might hope to survive. It was madness for Sattell to leave the ship.

"It doesn't make sense!" Borden said. "What has he to gain? He was afraid we'd go off and maroon him. We can't do that with crops going, the synthesizer working, and the drive pulled down. So what can he gain by running off?"

Ellen said uneasily, "Jerry's armed. And he won't be suspecting anything."

Borden scowled. "Get out the talkie and warn him. If Sattell surprises Jerry and gets his blaster, he might bushwhack us!"

Ellen brought out the talkie. She turned it on and said crisply: "Jerry, Sattell's disappeared. Come in please."

Jerry did not answer. Borden paced up and down, frowning and thinking of ever more disastrous possibilities.

"Bring the talkie into the ship," he said presently. "We'll hook it to an outside aerial. Jerry won't be traveling with his turned on. But he's bound to call us eventually."

He took the talkie from her, carried it inside the ship, and plugged it in there. In minutes a speaker in the control room was emitting the nondescript hissing which was the random electronic noises made by metal objects nearby. The ship itself, for one.

"I'm going to look in Sattell's cabin," said Borden grimly.

That was drastic action. On a space journey privacy is at once so difficult and so essential that nobody on a space expedition ever enters another's private cabin. To look in Sattell's cabin was a great violation of normal rules of conduct. But it had to be done now.

Borden went in the cabin and through Sattell's possessions. He came out looking sick.

"I found something," he told Ellen. "When we were coming in I looked at that white spot through a telescope. I didn't see anything worth noting, but I snapped the telecamera out of pure habit. Then I forgot it. But Sattell didn't. He made this."

He showed her a photographic print. Sattell had made it from the infra red image on the full color photograph. It was an enlargement, showing more detail than Borden had seen with the naked eye. There were shadows on this print, the shadows of structures. There were buildings rising from the white. There were towers. There was a city on the white spot from which a heat ray had been projected at the *Danaë* out in space!

Quite as important, the threadlike lines they had noticed were here plainly highways leading away from it. One led north, judging directions from the shadows. It reached toward the polar icecap near which the small space ship was grounded.

"If Sattell really expects us to kill him," said Borden, "he could have headed for that highway. He might expect to make a deal with our enemies by selling us out. Even if they killed him out of hand, the fact that he was an alien would make them hunt for us. So he could figure that he might make friends, but even if he didn't he would be sure to ruin us. A win for him either way."

Ellen paled a little. "And the drive's pulled down and Jerry's gone."

"So there's nothing to do but wait and see," said Borden.

He tried to work on the space drive. All its parts were spread out on the drive room floor. When they'd repaired it before, it had been so thoroughly fused that a part looked good even if repaired to the accuracy of a bent wax candle straightened out by hand.

Now the repairs looked very bad. It seemed incredible that anything so clumsily made should have worked. But Borden couldn't keep his mind on it.

"Just on the off chance, Ellen," he said abruptly, "you will not leave the ship by yourself. We'd better replace the lock door fastening, too. If we do have visitors from the city on the white spot, that won't stop them. But it might keep them from taking us off-guard."

He opened the thief-proof locker where an essential part of the lock catch had been stored, to protect it from Sattell. It had a combination fastening, intended merely to prevent pilfering when the ship was in a space port.

Borden reached in. Then he went completely and terribly white.

"He's got the star charts and the log! He got in here somehow!"

This was the ultimate in disaster. Because space is trackless. At fifty light years from Earth the Milky Way is still plain, of course, but the constellations have ceased to be. At a hundred light years one is lost. At a thousand light years—and the *Danaë* had passed that point months ago—a ship in space is in much the position of a canary whose universe has consisted of a cage in a single room, and has escaped out a window into the wide, wide world.

A space ship has to keep an infinitely precise log of bearings run and distances traveled in all three dimensions. It must make photographic star charts. And the accuracy of all its records must be perfect if it is to find the place it left nearly enough for the stars to become familiar again so it can locate the Solar System—barely four light hours in span.

"I think I made a serious mistake," Borden said quietly, "when I didn't kill Sattell!"

To find a spot four light years across in a galaxy a hundred thousand light years wide would be difficult enough with good maps. With no maps, they could spend the rest of their lives wandering hopelessly among the stars, of which not one in ten thousand had yet been named by men, landing on planets not one in a hundred thousand of which had known human footsteps. And they might search for months or years upon a planet where there was a human colony, and never discover its location.

Borden clenched and unclenched his hands. Sattell had been foisted upon him as a crew member while the *Danaë* was being fitted out for space. Borden was filled with a deadly cold fury in which regret for his own past forbearance was his principal emotion.

"Since he's taken the log and charts," he told Ellen icily, "he means either to bargain with us or to destroy us. And if I know Sattell, it's six of one and half a dozen of the other!"

It would be. Sattell now had the power of life and death over Borden and Ellen and Jerry. He would not trade that power for anything less. In fact, he would not dare yield it at all, because he was so sure he would be killed himself if he did. The only bargain he could conceivably make would be one in which they surrendered themselves to him absolutely, armed him and disarmed themselves, and threw themselves on Sattell's mercy. And Sattell had little mercy.

"You might try calling Jerry again," said Borden "Once we've warned him, we can try to track Sattell by his footprints. His shoes have heels, and the ground is soft."

Ellen picked up the walkie-talkie microphone again. "Jerry, Sattell's disappeared. Come in, please . . . Jerry, Sattell's disappeared. Come in, please . . ."

Her voice went on and on. Borden went grimly over the ship, looking for signs of what else Sattell might have busied himself with in the past twenty-four hours. He had believed that Sattell, being in the same boat with the rest of them—in the same space ship, anyhow—would automatically have thought of the group. No sane man did think of anything but cooperation with his companions in disaster.

But there exists a kind of human being, he knew, which may be a mutant, which makes a career of the gratification of all emotions, impulses, momentary desires. Which knows no purpose save personal satisfaction, and simply does not think like nonmutant human beings.

There were all too many specimens of this type among humans. Some ordinarily masked themselves, but if Satteil ever had, he now had been unmasked.

CHAPTER 4

ELLEN CALLED and called. Her voice grew weary and her shoulders drooped hopelessly as hours passed without reply.

Borden found where Sattell had crossed the wires so that if the ship took off and went out into space, the control board would show all air vents as safely sealed. But there would remain a small, steady drain of leakage of the ship's air stores.

He also found a small alteration of the water recovery system. They would have run out of water on the way home. He found a cunning circuit arranged so that if the ship rose on interplanetary drive and set out on even a hopeless search for home, the instant it went into overdrive its power tanks would fuse and short, and it would be left driveless and powerless, to crash or drift helplessly until its occupants died or went mad of despair.

Borden came back to the control room with his face set in savage lines.

"We didn't watch him," he said bitterly, "so he took advantage. Right now he's gloating, sure we have to accept any terms he demands, for the use of the log and maps to get home. And he's gloating because he'll have his revenge if we refuse, and if we do make a bargain he'll tell us how many ways we'd have died if we had not made it. We've got to check every device and every piece of equipment in the ship before we can lift off this planet—even after we've got fuel!"

He looked out a port. The shadows were long and slanting. It was twilight. Night was near.

Ellen said drearily into the talkie:

"Jerry, Sattell has vanished. Please come in! . . . Jerry, Sattell has vanished. Please come in!"

Far away, a tiny figure appeared in the half light. It came hastening toward the *Danaë*. It was one of the furry bipeds, probably one of those that had accompanied Jerry. It came through the dusk at an agitated lope, using its long, furry arms to balance itself. It made an agitated leap at sight of the space ship and rushed onward more frantically than before.

"Look!" cried Borden. "That looks like a messenger!" He went out the airlock door, his hand on the weapon in his holster.

The biped bounced at sight of him. Its fur flattened, but it came on at a tearing rush. It leaped and slid and came to rest before him, its trunk waving. He bent to scratch it, according to the custom that had become established in the past four days. But it did not wait. It stood up, making excited chirping noise and gesturing wildly. It made grimaces in the falling light.

Then Borden noticed blood on its fur.

* * * *

An hour later an almost unbearable bright light appeared in the distance, moving toward the *Danaë*. Jerry had carried a handflash, of course, but nothing equal to this. Judging by the wavering of the light, it was mounted on a vehicle of some sort.

Ellen's voice said wearily for the thousandth time: "Jerry, Sattell's vanished. Come in, please."

"You can stop that, Ellen," Borden told her. "The call's answered. It looks as if the real natives of this planet are coming to call."

He shrugged and turned to the furry creature which now was inside the ship. He'd bandaged its wound—a clean deep puncture in the flesh of its arm. He led it to the airlock.

"Get going," he said. "Your masters are coming. They won't like it that you've made friends with us. Scat!"

But the creature only blinked at the approaching light while its fur flattened. It went bouncing out and toward the swaying, lurching approaching light, racing joyfully to meet it.

Borden stared. Then he saw that other figures were about the approaching light beam—other furry, dancing, leaping creatures. They ran and gesticulated happily about the advancing vehicle.

It didn't make sense. But nothing did make sense on this planet!

Borden waited in the airlock, with Ellen behind him and a blaster in his hand. In the darkness the vehicle came lurching onward with surprising quiet. Its light swayed, and it had moved as if to turn, when Borden threw on the outside lights.

A semicircle of the sparse green vegetation sprang into brilliance. Borden and his wife were relatively in shadow. They could see the vehicle clearly.

It was nearly thirty feet long and rolled on two curious devices which were not caterpillar treads, but not exactly wheels, either. A loping, wildly excited horde of bipeds—including the one Borden had bandaged—surrounded it, making way for it but escorting it in wild enthusiasm.

The thing was caked with dirt. It was not merely dusty. It was packed with dried clay, as if it had been buried and only recently exhumed. A round blister at the front which might be plastic had been partly cleared of dirt, but there were still areas in which clay clung and made it opaque.

It curved about and swung parallel to the ship. It stopped within twenty feet of the airlock. Then an oval window—which looked as if somebody had scratched caked clay off it with a stick—turned endwise, quite impossibly, and became a door. The door slid aside. The interior of the vehicle was dark.

Borden held his blaster ready. He wouldn't shoot first, but there *had* been a heat ray flung at the *Danaë* . . .

And Jerry got out of the incredible vehicle and stood blinking embarrassedly in the light from the outerlock glare lamps.

Borden snapped, "Who's with you?"

"Why, nobody," said Jerry. "I tried to tell you by talkie, but it wouldn't work. I'm afraid Sattell did something to it before I left. It's dead."

"What's that thing?" demanded Borden. "That—that wagon?"

"It's a ground car, sir," Jerry said uncomfortably. "There are thirty or forty of them in a sort of valley about ten miles away. This one was half-buried in mud, and the others are the same or worse. The—er—creatures—took me there and dug this out for me. They apparently wanted us to have it."

"And it runs!" said Borden. There was again no sense to anything. A ground car buried in mud should not run when excavated.

"Yes, sir," said Jerry. "They dug it out for me, and I got in it and found the skeletons and the weapons."

Ellen said, "Skeletons?"

Borden said, "Weapons!"

"Yes, sir. I tried to ask you for advice over the talkie, and like I said, it wouldn't work, so I fiddled around a bit and the car showed signs of life, and I found out how to run it. So I brought it back. The weapons work too, sir. You point them at something and push a knob and they—well, they're pretty deadly."

Borden said flatly, "Sattell's ducked out. With the log and star maps and food. One of the creatures just came in wounded. I thought Sattell had planned to ambush you and get your blaster. If he did trail you—"

Jerry blinked, "I didn't see a sign of him. Just a moment, sir."

He turned to his furry companions. Flushing a little, he pulled something out of his pocket and hung it onto his chin. It was a sock—one of his socks—partly filled with clay.

Borden was still unable to find any two things happening on this planet which added together to make sense. The sight of Jerry fastening a clay-filled sock to his chin seemed slightly more insane than anything else that had happened.

"I've found out how they talk, sir," Jerry said shyly. "It's a sort of sign language with their hands and trunk, and they make noises for inflections and tenses, sir. And emotional overtones. I'm not too good yet, but—"

The scene before the lock door was unique. The clay-caked, thirty-foot vehicle looked more like a land yacht than a ground car. It was made of a golden metal. Two dozen or more of the furry bipeds were regarding Jerry as he made gestures and every so often stopped to adjust the position of his artificial trunk. When he made sounds at them, their fur flattened. When he adjusted his sock trunk, although it far from resembled their own, they seemed entranced. When he finished, the creature with the bandaged arm made elaborate gesticulations accompanied by chirping sounds. Even Borden, now that he had the key, gathered a dim idea of what the biped was trying to say.

"He says, sir," reported Jerry, sweating, "that a stick came through the air and stuck in his arm. He pulled it out and ran away. He kept on running. Then he saw this ship, ran to it, and you bandaged his arm for him."

Borden snapped, "An arrow! Sattell's made a bow and arrow. He sabotaged your talkie so you couldn't be warned about him, and he probably hoped to trail you and kill you with an arrow, so he could take your blaster and come back and kill us! Maybe he was just practicing when he hit this poor creature. Anyhow, he seems to be trying everything all at once, to destroy us." He added sharply, "But weapons! Jerry, from what you say there'll be more weapons in those other wagons! If he finds them, and he probably will, since he was trailing you—"

Jerry said, "I worried about that, sir. So I got the creatures to dig down to the doors of all the wagons in sight. I thought we'd better have the weapons safe before—er—Sattell tried to help us find out about the vehicles. I've got all the weapons right here. But there weren't weapons in all the wagons. In most of them there were just skeletons."

Borden was again reminded of the great number of things which did not fit together into any coherent picture. He said impatiently:

"Then Sattell won't get the weapons. But what's this you keep on saying about skeletons? Did you bring any of them?"

Jerry said, "I left those in here undisturbed. If you'll take the weapons as I hand them out, you can look them over. They're just as I first saw them."

He reached inside the vehicle, passed out objects midway between rifles and blasters in size. They were surprisingly light. They could have been aluminum, except that they were the color of gold or copper. There were three armsful of them.

Ellen took them inside and came back.

"Now I'll look at those skeletons," said Borden.

He took Jerry's hand flash and climbed inside. Jerry said apologetically to Ellen:

"I got so excited about what I found that I forgot about eating. Do you think I could fix something?"

"I'll do it for you, Jerry," said Ellen.

CHAPTER 5

SHE TOOK him inside. Sattell had carried away about most of the food in the current-use freezer, and the storage lockers were nearly empty, but she prepared an ample meal for him. She couldn't even guess at the significance of what he'd found, but she knew there was meaning to it if only it could be found.

Jerry was eating contentedly and telling Ellen about his journey with the furry bipeds when Borden came in. He went to a tool locker, got out a small torch, and went out again.

Considerably later the outer lock door clanked. Then Borden came back into the cabin where Jerry was still talking with his mouth full.

"I'm beginning to get an idea of what's happened on this planet," Borden said grimly. "Jerry, was there any sign of a highway where you found this bunch of wagons?"

Jerry considered: "The front part of this one," he offered finally, "was buried deeper than the back. It went into a sort of hill. And under the wheels there was flat stone. It could have been a highway, buried under the mud that partly covered up what you call the wagons, sir."

Borden nodded. "I've brazed the steering tiller of that wagon so it can't be steered," he observed. "And I've replaced the lock fastener so Sattell can't break into the ship. We can sleep tonight. Tomorrow we'll go over to those wagons and disable them all. And then, in this wagon you brought, we'll hunt Sattell down. I have an idea he'd better not have a wagon of his own. It might not be good for us."

Jerry asked rather breathlessly, "What did you think of the skeletons, sir? I left them exactly as they were." He hesitated. "I thought they were a lot like human skeletons. Is that right?"

"Quite right," agreed Borden. "There is an extra rib on each side, and three fewer vertebrae, and their joints were a little different, but they were people, as I interpret the word. Were there skeletons in all the wagons you entered?"

"Yes, sir."

Ellen said impatiently, "What did you find out, Dee?"

"I guessed," Borden told her. "But I'd bet on my guesses. For one thing, the group in this vehicle was a family. One was taller and stockier than the others. I could be wrong, but I think it was the male—the father. There is a slightly smaller, slightly slenderer skeleton there, too. It has jewelry on it. And there are two smaller skeletons." He took a deep breath. "The small skeletons were laid out neatly, comfortably. The next to largest skeleton was with them. The stocky skeleton . . . He'd killed himself, Jerry?"

"The weapons make holes like that, sir," said Jerry. "I tried one on the ground. Even in the ground cars where there were no weapons, one skeleton was always like that, with a hole in the skull."

"Yes," said Borden. "They must have loaned the weapons to each other for that purpose."

Ellen protested: "But Dee! What *was* it?"

"I've a pretty complete guess," Borden said evenly. "It includes Jerry's furry friends. They act like domestic animals, like pets with an inbred, passionate desire to be approved of by—people. Dogs are like that. You agree, Jerry?"

"Oh, yes, sir!"

"If a party of human beings, in flight from something dreadful, had come to some place in the arctic, on Earth, where they couldn't go any farther, where the wives and families they had with them had no chance of survival because of the thing from which they fled, what would they do?"

Jerry said awkwardly, "If I may say so, sir, it does look just like that!"

Borden went on without apparent emotion, "The men of those families would know there was no escape. The odds are that they'd put their family dogs out of the ground cars, because they might live. But if the situation was absolutely hopeless they might not want their families to suffer—what they'd first tried to escape. So the children would die painlessly. So would the women and then the men would kill themselves. Possibly, anyhow. Or they might go back and fight. Here, it seems, they killed themselves."

Ellen protested, "But what could be so hopeless? If the pets survived—"

"My guess doesn't run to what they fled from, Ellen. But I think it's the white spot that flung that heat ray at us. And I think that after all the people in the ground cars were dead, winter came, and covered up the vehicles with snow. Spring came, and floods washed mud along the highway and partly covered up the cars with mud. That went on for years and years and years. The pets that had been put out of the cars did survive. They were probably arctic animals to begin with, judging by their fur. And they have a language of sorts. They yearned for their masters. That was instinct. But they told their children—pups, what have you—about the masters they had lost. And one day a space ship came bumbling down out of the sky and landed with a crash—and Jerry got out of it. And he was like their masters. So they have adopted us as their masters. And so—that's my guess. All of it."

"Dee!" cried Ellen softly. "How terrible!"

"You think, sir," asked Jerry, "that they were running away from something on the white spot?"

"*We* did," said Borden. "We had to. Maybe they had to, too."

"But what do you think it is?"

"That," Borden told him," is something I hope we don't have to find out. Right now I suggest that we get some sleep."

And presently there was silence inside the *Danaë*, while the night grew deeper and darker outside.

There was no moon on this planet, but there were many stars in the sky. In the starlight the furry bipeds waited patiently about the hull for dawn when the humans would come out again. Some of them slept. Some sat erect, blinking meditatively. One or two walked about from time to time.

Occasionally one or more seemed to think there was a sound somewhere. They would look intently in the suspected direction until assured there was nothing amiss. They were much like dogs back on Earth, waiting hopefully for their masters to get up and be ready to pay attention to them again.

Hours later, the sky to the east paled. There was a chill mist to the northward, toward the polar cap. The ground in that direction glistened with the wet of condensation when the sky grew brighter. But here, so near the desert which save for the white spot covered the planet from pole to pole, there was no such excess of moisture. The ground here was damp because of seepage.

In a little while an eerie half-light spread over this curious world. The furry creatures sat up and scratched themselves luxuriously, and stretched in human fashion. Some of them scuffled amiably, tumbling over and over each other as if to warm themselves by exercise.

A little longer, and the sun rose. And shortly after that there were clankings when Borden unfastened the airlock and came out. Immediately he was the center of a throng of the bipeds, lying flat on theii backs with their stubby trunks waving urgently in the air, waiting to be scratched.

He scratched them gravely, one by one. Then Jerry came out and the process had to be repeated. The sun was low, and Jerry's shadow was thirty feet long on the sparsely covered ground.

Relieved of the biped's attentions, Borden moved off to one side. He had one of the stubby, golden-colored light metal weapons in his band. He examined it carefully, again.

There was a sort of stock, and a barrel three inches in diameter with an extremely tiny opening at its cnd. There was a round knob on one side. Borden unscrewed the knob a little, pointed the weapon carefully away from the *Danaë* and the furry creatures, and shifted the knob.

There was no noise. But what seemed to be a rod of flame shot out of the tiny muzzle. Where it touched the ground there was a burst of steam and flame and smoke from the scorched vegetation.

Borden turned it off quickly and aimed at a greater distance. He could not discover any limit to its range, in which respect it was a better weapon than the blaster of human manufacture he wore at his hip. It would be decidedly undesirable for Sattell to get hold of a weapon like this!

He went into the ship and when he came out again Ellen was with him. They put the golden metal weapons in the ground car. They brought out food. Ellen looked uneasily in the back, where she had heard there were skeletons, but they were gone. A mound of loosened soil nearby told where Borden had buried them, together.

"All set, Jerry?" asked Borden. "I've locked the ship so Sattell can't get in. As I told you, we're going to disable those other wagons and track down Sattell. If we can capture him reasonably intact, we'll put a cardiograph on him and ask him loaded questions about the ship's log and star maps. His pulse should change enough to enable us to track it down. But first we wreck those wagons!"

Jerry made gestures to his furry friends. They gesticulated back extravagantly. He climbed in the vehicle. Borden freed its tiller and Jerry drove.

For people effectively shipwrecked on an inimical planet and with no real hope of ever returning to their home, it was hardly appropriate that they got absorbed in the operation of a local vehicle. But this vehicle, large and roomy, was not a ground car so much as it was a land cruiser. It ran with astonishing smoothness, considering that it lacked pneumatic tires. And though from the outside it seemed to lurch and sway as it covered the rough ground, inside the lurchings were not felt at all.

The bipeds ran and skipped and loped beside it. Jerry picked up a little speed. They strained themselves to keep up.

Jerry had said ten miles. Actually, the distance was nearer twelve. There was snow in patches here and there.

The air grew misty. Through the mist the edge of the ice-cap could be seen, a wall of opaque white some sixty or seventy feet high at its rounded melting edge, and rising to greater thickness beyond. And they came to a small running stream some four or five feet wide. The first running water they had seen on this planet.

And there were the clustered vehicles, about forty of them lined up as if on a highway which had come to an end in an ice barrier now melted away.

The vehicles were partly or wholly covered with waterborne clay which had been laid upon them by just such meltings of the icecap. They ran on into a small hillock which had formed since they had come to a stop at this place. Some were merely hummocks of clay-covered metal, barely showing above the ground. Some were what could be called only hub deep in the clay. But it was being buried in the clay which had preserved them.

"You see, sir," Jerry explained, "I got the creatures to help me dig down to the doors, so I got into all that show. For weapons."

But Borden did not compliment him, though a compliment was due. Instead, Borden said in a toneless voice:

"I also see that Sattell has been here. He must have trailed you. He saw where you had driven one vehicle away. So he dug out the tracks of another one—there!— and tried it. And it worked. Sattell is gone."

It was true. Jerry, stricken, drove over to the new deep gouges in the earth which showed plainly where a way had been dug to take out another gold metal vehicle on its wheel-like treads, and that it had been backed from where it had been almost buried.

Bones on the ground showed where Sattell had savagely flung the pitiful relics of the original owners of the car. The prints of his boots were plain in the loosened dirt.

"We've got to chase him?" Ellen asked apprehensively.

"He has the star maps and the log," Borden said tonelessly. "Or else he knows where he hid them."

"But where would he go?" persisted Ellen.

"He knows we're after him," said Borden. "He knows we're armed, and I doubt that he is, except for his bow and arrow. Where would he go for help, except to the place where we have enemies?"

The track of the other vehicle was clear. There had been no feet heavier than those of Jerry's biped friends on any of this ground for many, many years. There was a deep furrow where the other ground car, the one Sattell had taken, had rolled away.

Jerry put on speed.

Borden said, "I'll watch how you drive this thing, Jerry, and relieve you presently. Sattell can't drive night and day. We can. And there's a long way to go. We'll catch him!"

But Sattell had a head start. Five miles from the beginning of the chase, the track they followed swung to the right and down a rolling hillside. They followed. And a seamless highway built of stone, patently artificial, came out of the hillside and stretched away across country.

It was forty feet wide. And here, in some dust that had drifted across it at some spots, they saw the trail of Sattell's car. At other places, even for most of the way, the winds had kept the roadway clear.

Jerry increased his speed. Borden thought to look at the road behind them.

Ellen, understanding, said, "No, the poor creatures couldn't keep up. They were running after us as if their hearts were breaking, but they couldn't make it."

Ten miles farther on, the highway was overwhelmed by wind-drifted sand. The trail of Sattell's fleeing car went up over the sand dune. They went after it. Half a mile farther, the highway was clear again. It swung south, headed out across the desert.

They did not catch sight of Sattell or his car.

For a stretch of twenty-five miles the arrow straight road was raised above the average level of the sands, and it was windswept. Then it went into a low range of rust-colored hills. Here they saw signs again of Sattell's passing. The streaked, rounded furrow of his vehicle's peculiar tread in windblown sand across the road.

On the far side of the hills they thought they had overtaken him when they saw the glint of golden metal a little off the highway.

They stopped. Borden and Jerry approached the spot, weapons ready. It was a ground car, past question, one like their own, but it had not been newly wrecked. That disaster had happened generations ago. The car had literally been pulled in half. It had been gripped by something unthinkably powerful and wrenched in two. The metal, strained and stretched before it broke, showed what had happened.

There were bones nearby. Not skeletons. Bones. Individual bones. Not gnawed. Not broken. Simply separated by feet and yards of space.

CHAPTER 6

SOME ten miles farther on they came to the first of the forts, a great, towering structure of rocks piled together across the road. It was a parapet sixty feet high, enclosing a square of space. In sheltered places among the rocks there was a vast amount of soot as if flames had burned here fiercely. But there was no charcoal. Here, too, were innumerable bones. There would have been thousands of skeletons in this walled area if they had been put together. But they were separate. Every bone, no matter how small, had been completely separated from every other bone.

They could be identified, however. These were the bones of people like those who once had owned this golden metal vehicle. They had died here by thousands. Weapons, bent and ruined, proved that they had died fighting. After death, each body had been exhaustively disjointed and the separate bones scattered utterly without system. And the victors had apparently done nothing else.

Borden knitted his brows as the ground car went on, having perilously skirted around the walls. Jerry seemed to feel that he had wasted time looking. He tried a higher rate of speed. The car yielded it without effort. There seemed to be no limit to the speed at which these remarkable vehicles could travel without vibration or swaying or jolting.

That first fort was perhaps fifty miles behind when Borden's expression changed from harried bewilderment to shock. He stared ahead as the vehicle sped along the geometrically linear highway, windswept and free of dust as it was.

He said slowly, "That's right, Jerry. Make as much speed as you can. When you're tired, I'll drive. We've got to catch Sattell before he reaches that white spot. It's possible that more than our lives depend on it . . ."

They did not catch Sattell, though they drove night and day. Their speed varied from fifteen miles an hour when they crawled over occasionally drifted sand dunes which swallowed the highway, to two hundred miles an hour or better. Borden estimated grimly that they averaged more than a thousand miles per twenty-hour day.

Sattell couldn't have kept that up, so they must have passed him, probably as he slept in some hiding place off a rocky spot in the highway where there would be no trail to guide them to him. But of course the wind might have erased his trail anywhere.

Ellen tried to rest or doze in the back while Jerry or Borden drove on, one resting while the other drove. But after the first day the actual overtaking of Sattell plainly was not Borden's purpose. It was clear that he meant to get ahead of Sattell, to reach the white spot first.

On the second day of their journeying they found a second fort. This also was a structure across the highway, defended from attack in the direction for which they were headed. It had been more carefully built than the other one. This had been more constructed of squared stones, lifted into position by construction engines whose sand-eroded carcasses were still in place.

There also were larger instruments of warfare here, worn away by centuries of exposure to blowing sand. The fort itself had many times been filled with sand and emptied again by the wind. Only under archways were there any signs of soot, as if flames had burned terribly here. Some land cruisers such as the one in which they rode had been destroyed like the one they had seen at the first fort—pulled apart.

Like the other fort this one had not been demolished after its capture. Not even the cranes and weapons had been seized. But the defenders had been completely dismembered. No two bones were ever attached to each other. Rarely had one been broken. None had been gnawed. Some were sand-worn, but each was complete and entirely separate.

And tens of thousands—not merely thousands—had died here. Their bones proved it.

Ellen watched Borden's face as they drove through this fortress.

"Do you know what happened, Dee?" she asked.

"I think so," he said coldly.

"The white spot? It looks as if they had been fighting something that came from there."

"They were," said Borden. "And I don't want Sattell to encounter the thing they were fighting. He knows too much."

She studied his expression. She knew that they were making the top possible speed toward that same white spot from which a heat ray had been thrown at them. He hadn't explained. Jerry was too diffident to ask. Ellen was not, but something occurred to her suddenly.

"You said, the 'thing'!" she said, startled. "Not creatures or people or anything like that! You said the thing!"

He grimaced, but did not answer her. Instead, he said, "I'll take the tiller, Jerry. We've still got the talkie that Sattell sabotaged, haven't we?"

Jerry nodded and shifted the tiller to him. They'd discovered that the steering gear could be shifted from side to side of the front of the vehicle, so that it could be driven from either the right or left side. On a planet without cities but with highways running thousands of miles to the polar icecaps, long distance driving would be the norm. Conveniences for that purpose would be logical. Drivers could relieve each other without difficulty.

"Look it over," commanded Borden. "The logical way to sabotage a talkie would be to throw its capacitances out of balance. No visible sign of damage, but I couldn't find a band it wasn't tuned to. See if that was the trick."

Jerry busied himself as Borden drove on. Here the highway wound through great hills, the color of iron rust and carved by wind and sand into incredibly grotesque shapes. A long trail of swirling dust arose behind the racing cruiser.

Borden said abruptly, "I've been thinking. Check me, will you two? First, I think the people who made this vehicle were much like us. The skeletons proved that. They had families and pets and they made cars like this to travel long distances on highways they'd built from pole to pole. This car uses normal electric power, and its power source is good! So they should have had radio frequency apparatus as well as power. But no radio frequency is being used on this planet. The race that built this car, then, has either changed its culture entirely, or been wiped out."

Jerry said blankly, "You mean, the people in the white spot—"

"Are not, and were not the race that built the roads and made this machine," said Borden. "In fact, we've passed two forts where people like us died by tens of thousands, fighting against something from the white spot. They had long range weapons, but at the end they were fighting with fire. You saw the soot! It was as if they burned oil by thousands of gallons to hold back something their long range weapons couldn't stop. Fire is a short-range weapon, though a sun mirror need not be. But nothing stopped this enemy. Vehicles like this were pulled right in half. That doesn't suggest people. It suggests a thing—something so gigantic and horribly strong that needle beams of flame couldn't stop it, and against which flame seemed a logical weapon to use. It must have been gigantic, because it could pull a land car apart endwise."

Ellen waited. Jerry knitted his brows. "I'm afraid," Jerry said, "I can't think of anything that would be that big and I just can't think what they could have been fighting."

"Think of what it wanted," Borden said drily. "It killed the population, wiped them out. Back on Earth, a long, long time ago, Ghenghis Khan led the Mongols to destroy Kharesmia. His soldiers looted the cities. They carried away all the wealth. They murdered the people. Plains were white with the skeletons of the folk they murdered. Do you notice a difference here?"

Jerry said irrelevantly, "You were right about the talkie, sir. Somebody's thrown it all out of tuning. I'll have to match it with the other to make use of it." Then he said painstakingly, "The difference between what you mentioned and the conquerors of the forts is that the loot was left in the forts. Engines and weapons and so on weren't bothered." Then he said in sudden surprise, "But the people weren't left as skeletons! They were all scattered!"

Jerry raised startled eyes from the talkie on which he was working. And suddenly he froze. Borden braked, stopped the car. They had come to a place where shattered ground cars were on the highway, on the sides of the road, everywhere. Here the road ran between monstrous steep-sided hills.

Borden started the car again and drove carefully around half of a vehicle which lay on the highway. Weapons had been mounted in it for shooting through the blister that was like the blister through which he looked in their car.

"There was a battle here, too," he said. "They fought with cars here. Maybe a delaying action to gain time to build the fort we just left. There are bones in these cars, too."

"But what were they fighting, Dee?" Ellen demanded again, uneasily.

Borden drove carefully past the scene of ancient battle—and defeat. He did not answer.

After a time Ellen said, more uneasily still, "Do you mean that whatever they fought against was—going to eat them? It wanted their—bodies?"

"So far as we can tell," said Borden, "it took nothing else. Didn't even want their bones."

He drove on and on. He didn't elaborate. There was no need. A creature which consumed its victims without crushing them or biting them or destroying the structure of their bones! It must simply envelop them. Like an amoeba. A creature which discarded the inedible parts of its prey in separate fragments, without order of position, without selection. That also must be like an amoeba which simply extrudes inedibles through its skin. Ellen swallowed suddenly and her eyes looked haunted.

"Something like a living jelly, Dee," she said slowly. "It would flow along a highway. If you shot it with a needle ray, it wouldn't stop because it would use the burned parts of its own body as food. You'd think of burning oil as a way to fight it. You'd try to make forts it couldn't climb over. Where would such a thing come from, Dee?"

Borden said drily, "From space. Maybe as a spore of its own deadly race. Or it might be intelligent enough for space-travel. It should be! It knew enough to make a sun mirror of itself to destroy us! It also knew enough to make itself into straining cables to pull ground cars like this apart to get at the people inside."

Ellen shuddered. "But that must be wrong, Dee! A creature like that would cover a whole planet! It would consume every living thing and become itself the planet's surface or its skin."

"But this planet is mostly desert," Borden reminded her. "It may be that there was just one oasis on which a civilization started. Sun power was all it had. It would make use of that. It would find the icecaps at its poles, and build highways to them to haul water to extend itself. Its people would delight in such strangeness as running streams, like the one we saw. If something hellish came out of space, landed, and attacked that oasis, the thing would follow the survivors of its first attacks along the highways by which they retreated. When they built forts, they would congregate in numbers it could not resist attacking. And—"

Jerry glanced up. His face was white, and he looked sick.

"I recall, sir," he murmured, "that you said Sattell knew too much. I believe you guess the 'thing' you are talking about absorbed the knowledge of the people it consumed. Is that right? And if it should absorb more from Sattell, and through him know about us—"

"My guess," said Borden, "is that it knew we were in a space ship. In one there are always relays working, machines running, things happening—as is always the case where there are humans. Where there are living beings. Such happenings can be detected. I also believe this 'thing' can tell when it can reach the living, and when it can't. When it can reach them, it undoubtedly moves to devour them. When it can't it tries to destroy them—as it tried with us. That may be because of its own intelligence, or it may be because of the knowledge gained through what it has consumed.

"That's why I don't intend to let Sattell be consumed by it! He knows how the *Danaë*'s drive works and how it should be repaired. He knows how to read the log and the maps he stole. Just as a precaution, I'm not going to let that 'thing' in the white spot gain the knowledge that there is a planet called Earth with life all over it, on every continent, and in the deeps of the seas. *If* the 'thing' in the white spot were to find out that there is such a place, and *if* it is intelligent enough to wipe out a civilized race on this planet, it might be tempted to take to space again. Or at least to send, say, part of itself!"

CHAPTER 7

ABRUPTLY the wind-carved, rust-colored hills came to an end. The highway curved slightly and reached out toward the horizon. But the horizon was not, now, a mere unending expanse of dunes and desert.

A bare few miles distant, the desert was white. There were no dunes. A vast, vast flat mass of nothing-in-particular, not even raising the level of the ground, reached away and away to this world's edge. It looked remarkably like a space on which a light snowfall had descended, shining in the sunlight until melting should come. The towers of the city in the midst of it also were shimmering white.

But it all was not a completely quiescent whiteness. There were ripplings in it. A pinnacle rose abruptly, and Borden backed the vehicle fiercely as the pinnacle formed a cuplike end of gigantic size, and the interior of that cup turned silvery.

The rust-colored hills blotted out just as a beam of purest flame licked from it to the spot where the ground car had been the moment before. Rocks split and crackled in the heat.

The beam faded. The light vanished.

"So," said Borden matter-of-factly, continuing what he had been saying, as if there had been no interruption, "as long as Sattell is at large, why, we have to kill that 'thing.' I think I know how to do it. With a little overload, I believe that walkie-talkie will do the trick. You see, the 'thing' is terrifically vulnerable, now. It has conquered this planet. It was irresistible. Nothing could stand against it. So it will be easy to kill."

But in that opinion, Borden was mistaken. Living creatures moving toward the white spot should have had no reason to be suspicious. Traveling at high speed along the highway, they should have continued at high speed to the very border of the white spot, at least. More probably they should have entered the white-covered area filled with a mild curiosity as to what made it so white. And of course the white spot—the horror, the protean protoplasm of which it was composed—would have engulfed them. But the car stopped. And the white spot was intelligent.

* * * *

Twenty minutes after the first crackling impact of a heat beam in the valley, Borden was out of the ground car and moving carefully to peer around a rocky column at the white spot.

Its appearance had changed. There was a rise in the ground level at the edge of the white spot now. The stuff which was the creature itself—which Ellen had aptly called a living jelly—had flowed from other places to form a hillock there. Borden regarded it with suspicion. Obviously, it could send out pseudopods. Amoebae can do that, and he had just seen this thing form a sun ray projector of itself.

But Borden was not aware of the possibilities of a really protean substance to take any form it desires.

He saw the pseudopod start out. He was astounded. It did not thrust out. The hillock, the raised-up ground level, suddenly sped out along the highway with an incredible swiftness. He regarded it with a shock that was almost paralyzing.

But not quite. He fled to the car, leaped into it, and sent it racing down the highway at the topmost speed he could coax from it. His face was gray and sweating. His hands shook.

Ellen gasped, "What, Dee? What's happened?"

"The beast," said Borden in an icy voice. "It's after us."

Ellen stared back. And she saw the tip-end of the white spot's pseudopod as it came racing into the end of the valley through which the highway ran. It was a fifty-foot, shapeless blob of glistening, translucent horror. And it did not thrust out from the parent body. It laid down a carpet of its own substance over which its fifty-foot mass slid swiftly.

An exact, if unimpressive, analogy would be a cake of wet soap, or a mass of grease, sliding over a space it lubricated with its own substance as it flowed, leaving a contact with its starting point as a thin film behind. Or it could be likened to a roll of carpet, speeding forward as it unrolled.

A hillock of glistening jelly, the height of a five-story building, plunged into the valley at forty miles an hour or better. By sheer momentum it flowed up the mountain-side, curved, and came sliding back to the highway and on again after the ground car.

But the car was in retreat at over a hundred miles an hour. It reached a hundred and fifty miles an hour. Two hundred.

Borden stopped it five miles down the highway and wiped his forehead.

"Now," he said grimly, "I see why ordinary weapons didn't work against it. The thing is protean, not amoeboid. It isn't only senseless jelly. It has brains!"

He considered, frowning darkly. Then he turned the ground car off the road. He drove it around a dune, and another. It became suddenly possible to see across the desert toward the white mass at the horizon.

There was a ribbon, a road, a highway of whiteness leading toward the city. The five-story-high mass of stuff that had come sweeping toward the car had traveled along the highway, carpeting the rocky surface with its own substance. Now there were new masses of loathsome whiteness surging along the living road. There were billows, surgings, undulations. It was building up for a fresh and irresistible surge.

Across the desert a new pseudopod, a new extension of the white organism, moved with purposeful swiftness. It was somehow like a narrow line of whitecaps moving impossibly over aridness.

"It knows we stopped," Borden said. "It won't attack. It'll act as if baffled—until there's a fresh mass of it behind us. Then it will drive together and catch us in between. Jerry, are you set to try the talkie stuff?"

"Pretty well,", sighed Jerry.

The car crawled back to the highway. The waiting mass of jellylike monster was larger. It grew larger every instant, as fresh waves of its protaean substance arrived through the throbbing of the pseudopod back to the oasis.

"Turn on the walkie-talkie," commanded Borden.

Jerry, white and shaken, threw the switch. An invisible beam of microwaves sped down the valley behind the halted car. It reached the blob of jelly which now was as large as when it had started from the parent mass. The jelly quivered violently. Then it was still.

"Turn it off," ordered Borden. "Why didn't that work?"

Jerry turned off the microwave beam. The jelly quivered once more. Borden, watching with keen eyes, said: "On again."

The pile of jelly quivered a third time, but less violently. The first impact of the microwave beam had bothered it, but it had been able to adjust almost instantly. It perceived the microwaves. That much was certain. But it could adjust to them.

Borden said furiously, "The thing can learn! It can think. It is smart as the devil! But if I am right, what it wants more than anything else is not to do anything. It has to be awake, when we are near. It can't help itself, but it wants to sleep. We and our microwaves are like mosquitos buzzing around a man's head. I thought they—"

He stopped short, but after a moment laughed unpleasantly.

"I get it. When it learns a pattern it can disregard it. Living things always act without pattern. So it can't disregard them. But it could disregard an unmodulated beam. Let's see what a modulated one will do. Jerry, the microphone."

When the talkie went on and its beam of microwaves hit the monstrous, featureless thing, it did not even quiver. Then Borden said into the microphone:

"'Mary had a little lamb. Its fleece was white as snow. And everywhere that Mary went—'."

The monstrous mass of ghastly jelly plunged toward him.

Ellen shot the ground car away. Borden's throat contracted. When his voice stopped, the frenzied movement of the horror ceased. It stood trembling in a gigantic, glistening heap. It seemed to wait.

Borden considered it grimly.

"It could make a sun mirror now," he decided, "but not a very big one. We'd run away. It doesn't want to chase us away until that other arm of stuff gets behind us. If we run, it will follow. It could follow the original inhabitants of this planet for thousands of miles. Doubtless it would follow us as far.

"And there's always Sattell. We've got to kill it. How? I thought a walkie-talkie beam would irritate it. It can adjust to it. Then I thought a modulated wave—voice-modulated—would exhaust it. But no. We need something new, right now!"

There was silence. Then Ellen said uneasily:

"Maybe this idea isn't sensible, but could it be that the walkie-talkie beam just wasn't strong enough? It was too much like—like tickling it, arousing its appetite. Maybe if the beam were powerful enough it would be like paralysis."

Borden did not even answer. He hauled at the objects that had been found to be the covers to the power leads of the vehicle. He and Jerry worked feverishly, without words. Then Borden stood up.

"This time we are really risking everything," he said. "The full power of the car's power source goes into the beam. If a walkie-talkie beam was appetizing, this ought to curl its hair. Switch, Jerry! Microphone on!"

CHAPTER 8

SOME hundreds of kilowatts of power in modulated wave form would go out now into the body of a creature whose normal sensory reception centers would be accustomed to handling minute fractions of one watt. The talkie could handle the power, of course. With cold-emission oscillators, there was no danger of burning out a wave-generating unit.

"'—the lamb was sure to go,'" said Borden.

The two-mile distant mass of horrid jelly began to quiver uncontrollably. But without any purpose at all. Borden said with a terrible satisfaction:

"'It followed her to school one day, which was against the rule. It made the children laugh and play to see the lamb at school.'"

The shapeless mass of living stuff made tortured upheavals. It flung up spires of glistening stuff. It writhed. It contorted. It flung itself crazily against the hillsides.

"''Twas brillig,'" said Borden, "'and the slithy toves, did gyre and gimble in the wabe. All mimsy were the borogoves, and the mome raths outgrabe.'"

The jelly fled. It flowed back upon the carpet of its own substance on which it had been able to move with such ghastly speed. It flowed down from a mound to a flattened thickening of the pseudopod which had thrown itself at the car.

That pseudopod flowed away upon itself. It fled. It raced frantically to be gone from a beam of microwaves whose pattern was not fixed, which varied unpredictably from instant to instant as sound waves changed it from something the white spot being could disregard to something which did not promise food, and which could not be ignored.

The white spot creature was tormented. Its instincts said that what was not patterned was life. Its intelligence said that this was not life—not life in quantity proportional to the stimulus, it yielded, anyhow. The modulated microwaves impressed its consciousness as a steam whistle at his ear impresses a man. The sensation was intolerable. It was maddening.

In less than an hour, Borden had returned to the end of the valley and was beaming microwaves at the white spot across the few miles of desert in between. He was beginning to be weary now, and his memory for recitative verse was running thin.

"Take over and keep talking, Ellen," he said into the microphone. He handed it to her.

Ellen said steadily, "I don't know how this is doing what it does, but—'My name is John Wellington Wells, I'm a dealer in magic and spells, in hexes and curses and ever-filled purses and witches and crickets and elves.' I've got this wrong somehow, Dee, but tell me what it is and I'll try to keep on."

Borden said, "I'd rather not tell you. It would overhear. I think, though, that it's moving away. The white stuff is drawing back!"

And it was true. The whiteness which had been beyond the desert was withdrawing. The pseudopod—a misnomer, because in this case the word should have been something else—the extension which had come to destroy the humans had long since withdrawn. The formless ground-covering was gathering itself into a mass, and that mass was moving away.

There was a dark space visible. It was ground—humus, oasis soil—which had been covered by the unspeakable organism which centuries since had conquered this planet.

"I'd chase it," Borden said somberly, "only I'm not sure it couldn't get itself together and make a sun mirror. We'll wait till nightfall."

"But what are we doing to it?" demanded Ellen.

Jerry was at the microphone now, going through the *Sonnets from the Portuguese*, while the living jelly at the edge of the world quivered and fled in shaking revulsion.

"The thing's alive," said Borden. "And it can't help receiving all sorts of impressions. Like any other organism, it learns to disregard any impression it receives that it can anticipate or classify. We don't hear a clock ticking. If we live near a noisy street, we don't hear traffic. But we wake if a door squeaks. That—white spot can disregard the electric waves of lightning. It can disregard sunshine. But it can't disregard things it can't fit into a pattern. It has to pay attention. And I'm giving it the kind of unpatterned signals that normally mean living things. Continuous, nonrepeat patterns of stimulation. And—they're too strong for the devilish thing."

Ellen said doubtfully, "Too strong?"

"You touch people to call their attention. If you touch them too hard, it isn't a touch but a blow, and you can knock them down. That's what I'm giving this thing. It has the quality of a signal the spot can't ignore, and the force of a blow. It should have the psychological effect of thousands of bells of intolerable volume—only worse. But we've got to keep on with the stimulus. And we mustn't repeat, or it might be able to get used to the pattern."

"I'll talk to it in French," said Ellen. "But it doesn't seem to me that a walkie-talkie could be too strong for—"

"It's hooked to the car's power system," Borden told her. "Jerry set it up and connected it just before he began to recite poetry. There are several kilowatts of radiation going to the thing now, and all of it is attention-holding radiation."

* * * *

When night fell and the use of a sun mirror was patently impossible, Borden moved on the highway toward what had been the white spot. The walkie-talkie sent on its waves ahead.

Ellen recited, *"La fourmi et la cigale"* from second-year French. Borden was more or less ready to take on from there with what he remembered of Shakespeare.

They reached the end of the desert and all about them there was the moist ground of the oasis which once had been the center of a civilization. Presently they moved into the deserted, emptied buildings of a city.

Borden said, "This civilization will be worth studying!"

They went on and on and on, talking endlessly, and driving the entity which had conquered a planet by painstakingly recalled sections of Mother Goose, and by haphazard recollections of ancient history, the mythology of ancient Greece and Rome, and the care and feeding of domestic cats.

When dawn came, Borden was speaking rather hoarsely into the microphone, and the creature was plainly in sight before them. It writhed and struggled spasmodically. It flung masses of itself insanely about. It knitted itself into intricate spires and pinnacles, with far-flung bridges, which shuddered and dissolved.

* * * *

The sun rose, and the thing should have been able to destroy them. But it could not. It still writhed. It still shuddered. It twisted in monstrous, weary, lunatic gyrations. Ellen regarded it with eyes of loathing.

"It acts like it's gone mad," she said in revulsion.

"It may have," said Borden. "It's certainly exhausted. But we're getting pretty tired, too." He said into the microphone. "You probably don't understand this that I'm saying, any more then you understand any of the rest. But you had this coming to you."

He handed the microphone to Jerry, who had suddenly remembered an oration, *Spartacus to the Gladiators*.

Jerry began to recite it.

But the writhings of the mountainous mass of jelly became more terribly weary, more quiveringly effortful. There came a time when it quivered only very, very faintly. Those quiverings ceased.

"I think it's dead, sir," said Jerry.

Borden snapped off the walkie-talkie. He snapped it on again. The horrible, half cubic mile of jelly did not flinch.

Borden said drily, "Abracadabra, hocus pocus, e pluribus unum."

There was no sign of life in the thing. He watched grimly for any sign of returning activity. By noon, though, it could be seen that the ghastly mass of once-living substance was changing. It was liquefying. There were rills of an unpleasant fluid forming on its glossy flanks, to run down and flow and flow away into the desert to be dried up.

"I don't think we'll want to be around for the next few weeks," Borden said heavily. "We'll go back and fix up the ship."

Then Ellen mentioned Sattell's name for the first time in days.

"How about Sattell?"

"We outran him on the way here," Borden said moodily. "But I think he'll come on. He'll want to find out if we're dead. Not knowing what the thing—the white spot—was, I think he'll figure that either we'll be sent back with help, or killed. If he gets to where he can see the white spot, and we haven't started back with friends, he'll be sure we're dead. Then he'll go back and start to fix up the ship himself. I think we'll meet him on the way."

And they did. The second day out from what was now an oasis instead of a white spot, they saw Sattell's car headed in their direction as a moving gleam of golden reflected sunlight.

Jerry ran their car off the road to a hiding-place behind a dune. He and Borden took posts behind the sand dune's tip. Sattell came racing at a hundred and fifty miles an hour, raising a long plume of sand dust behind him.

Borden and Jerry fired together—two thin pencil rods of flame from the golden-metal weapons. Sattell's ground car ran past them, crossing the highway just a foot from the rock. The treads of the car disintegrated. The car sped on, slid, and rolled clumsily, three separate times. Then it stopped.

The oval side window turned and Sattell came crawling out. He had a golden-metal weapon now. He must have searched feverishly in the shambles of one of the two forts to find a weapon that still would operate. He swung it frenziedly in their direction. He ran toward them, screaming hate. He stumbled.

His weapon was firing, but the fire was short. He fell on it. Into its flame.

And the ship's log and the star maps were in the ground car Borden and Jerry had disabled.

* * * *

It was more than a month later when the *Danaë*, completely overhauled and refueled, and with the product of Ellen's agriculture stored carefully away, hovered cautiously over what had been the white spot. At last they descended into the central square of the city that once had been the center of a civilization.

The three of them spent a day examining that city. They found things they could not understand, and things at which they smiled, and things that were quite marvelous. Every civilization makes some discoveries that others miss, and misses that others take for granted. There would be useful items in this civilization, when humans landed here and examined the remains.

"I think," Ellen said, to Borden, "that you mean to come back."

Borden nodded, frowning a little.

"No rational natives," he said, "and eighteen thousand square miles of oasis. It would make a rather wonderful place in which to live—with that city and that civilization to study. Will you mind?"

Ellen laughed. She held out her hand. There were capsules in it.

"I've been planting more seeds," she said, "so there'll be Earth-type vegetation here when we get back."

"And Jerry?"

Jerry said bashfully, "There's a girl . . . If I can organize a group to make a settlement here, I think I'll be back."

"Then we'll be back," said Borden. "And next time we'll bring some of our furry friends down from the ice-cap and really find out what it means to settle down and live here."

And then the *Danaë* climbed for the stars and started back home.

www.ingramcontent.com/pod-product-compliance
Lightning Source LLC
Chambersburg PA
CBHW020650130626
46552CB00003B/1484